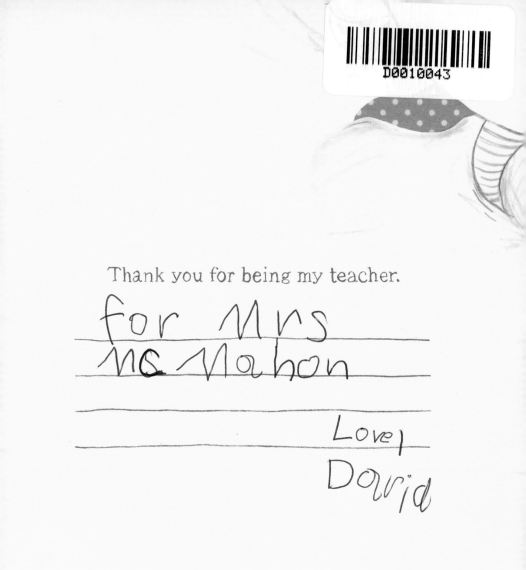

Thank you for being my teacher.

for Mrs
mc Mahon

Love,
David

Because I Had a Teacher

Written by Kobi Yamada   Illustrated by Natalie Russell

Because I had a teacher,
I love to learn.

I discovered that I can do much
more than I thought I could.

I realized it's okay when some
things are harder than others.

I found that challenges can be fun.

Because I had a teacher,
I discovered that there are
lots of ways of being smart.

And I know that mistakes are
just part of getting something right.

I realized that some of the
hardest things for me to do
make me feel the proudest.

Because I had a teacher,
I know how good it feels when
someone is happy to see me.

I know that I can always ask for help.

I feel like I have a friend on my side.

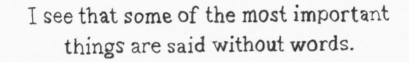

I see that some of the most important things are said without words.

Because I had a teacher,
I have whole new worlds to explore.

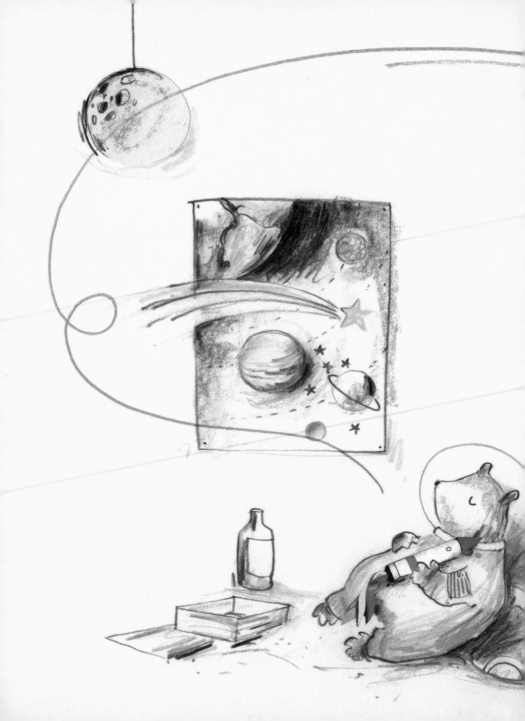

I discovered that what I can
imagine, I can make real.

And now I feel like I can do anything.

Because I had you,
I learned to believe in me.

COMPENDIUM.
live inspired

Thank you to Mr. Gotchy. A truly extraordinary teacher. ~K.Y.

To Maxine—an amazing teacher! ~N.R.

Written by: Kobi Yamada
Illustrated by: Natalie Russell
Edited by: Amelia Riedler, M.H. Clark, and Ruth Austin
Designed by: Sarah Forster

Library of Congress Control Number: 2016945645 | ISBN: 978-1-943200-08-5

16th printing. Printed in China with soy inks on FSC®-Mix certified paper. A032210016

*Create
meaningful
moments
with gifts
that inspire.*

CONNECT WITH US
live-inspired.com | sayhello@compendiuminc.com

@compendiumliveinspired
#compendiumliveinspired